JAILAA WEST

Cherishing Her

First edition

This book was professionally typeset on Reedsy. Find out more at reedsy.com

Contents

Acknowledgement

Dear Reader,

Thank you so much for allowing me to share my story with you. I sincerely hope you enjoy this book as much I enjoyed writing it. Cherishing Her is book One in the Skin Sins Tattoo Shop series. These books can be read independently. However, I believe it so much fun to check in on all of the other character's lives. If you would like to read about the other characters. Please visit the series web page. But for now, sit back, relax and enjoy!

Books by Jailaa West

Savage Security Series
Submit (Prequel)
Obey
Control
Lauren
Yield
Thalia
Bound
A Savage Christmas Wedding

Savage Security: The Ismailovs
Taken by the Bratva Prince

Skin Sins Tattoo Shop Series
Cherishing Her
Choosing Her
Coveting Her
Craving Her
Completing Her
Skin Sins: An MC Romance Box Set (Vol 1)
The Biker Takes a Bride (Part of the *After I do* series)

Dentown Shifter Series
Laid Bear

Forever After
Yours Until Midnight (included in the Kwanzaa
Kisses collection)
Loving the Beast

Southern Charms and Farms
Dad Bod Country Boy (Included in the Dad Bod
Collection)
The Bookworm and the Bad Boy (Coming Soon!)

Cherishing Her

Chapter 1

Rogue put down his gun and watched her walk into the shop. Shit, she was back. He remembered the dark-haired beauty from her last visit. Hell, you didn't forget a woman like Marley. A woman who snatched your heart out of your chest and then left with it.

"Is everything okay? How did it turn out?" He'd spent hours working on her tattoo, long after the shop would have closed for anybody else.

His brothers had knocked on the door to make sure they were okay. But they knew better than to open it when Rogue was working. He'd given her a masterpiece. It had been a sin and a shame to cover it up. He'd wanted to wrap her in silk instead of bandages. Carry her home in his arms and provide her with aftercare. Watch his art bloom into life as she healed. Instead, she'd taken the canvas of his best art home. Alone. Her eyes had glistened, and she'd mumbled thank you as if magic hadn't sprung between them. As if only he knew she was his. It had taken a boatload of strength to let her go. And now she was back. Did she expect him to let her go again? She shrugged. "It's fine. Everything turned out okay, but I'm thinking of getting more."

"More?" Shit, how much more would he have to give?

Each needle that pierced her beautiful brown skin punctured his heart. Every time she'd winced, he'd cursed and apologized. It was a lot of damn cursing. Now she wanted more. The only reason he hadn't stopped before was that he didn't want her leaving with a fucked up half-tatt. So, he'd continued. Cursing himself to hell and back.

"More?" He repeated like a damn fool. When he wanted to say *hell no*.

"Not more ink."

He gave a relieved sigh as she lifted her eye. Meeting his steady gaze for the first time.

Her brows drew together. "You think I can't take more ink?"

"It's not that..." he shook his head. "But last time, you were in a lot of pain. We had to go deep to make sure it took past the scarring."

She gave a little wince and slid her eyes away again. Torturing him with their removal.

"I didn't think you'd be back so soon. I thought you did everything you wanted last time."

She folded her hands across her chest. "Do you

2

have any idea what I wanted?"

He shook his head. He'd figured it wasn't a simple tattoo. Many clients used their tattoo artists as counselors. Spilling out their guts while he worked. Especially when they worked through the night. He'd never worked on a client who'd been so silent. But by the end of the night, he knew her better than any client he'd ever had. As if they'd been soldiers in a battle locked in silence through a long night, waiting for the enemy to retreat.

Her steady strength, even during the most painful moments, said a lot. And the scars he'd covered said even more. What had she really wanted? The hell if he knew. He only saw the courage she'd displayed in getting it. And courage meant a hell of a lot in his world. Cause bravery wasn't always the man willing to hold a gun and fire. A lot of damn times, bravery meant walking away while under fire.

That's what Ruiz, the former leader of the Roarers, had done. Walked away and took the fall so that the rest of them could survive. They owed him their lives. Brothers forever bound by his sacrifice. They'd each taken a biker name, starting with the letter 'R', to honor him. But it wasn't enough, never would be. So, they'd vowed to go straight. Every single Roarer left the life. Vowing to never commit another crime. To never let Ruiz's sacrifice be in vain. Moving away to a small town and opening a tattoo shop because hell, what else did they know how to do?

"I thought you wanted your scars covered." He waved a hand to her chest.

Her eyes glistened, and she glared at him. A kitten spitting fire. Making him harder than a gun barrel.

"It was never about the scars." She thumped her chest. "It was about me getting back to being me." She waved her hand up and down over her chest. "People keep congratulating me on being a survivor. 'You survived breast cancer.' Whoop, whoop. I ended my last round of medications and have been cancer-free for five years. Another shake, dance, and party. Again, whoop, whoop. But I still don't feel like me. They sliced off my breasts, something I gave up willingly. Grateful to have a chance at surviving. No one told me, that five years later, I would feel less. I still can't look in the mirror and feel beautiful."

When he gave a sharp intake, she snapped her eyes at him, but he couldn't help it. She was so beautiful and could turn a man into a pillar of salt with a glance. She couldn't see that? Didn't feel that? What the fuck? Was she shitting him or having a pity party? She wasn't the type. Not with the way she had handled getting inked. Even when an occasional tear had slipped down the side of her face. She'd given a silent nod when he'd asked her if he should keep going. She was speaking her truth, but he had to shut that shit down.

"You're more beautiful than the sun rising over a desert horizon. More beautiful than the moon, glowing on a starless night. More beautiful than waves breaking against an ocean cliff..." His words trailed off when she stood with her mouth open.

He'd said too much. Sounded like a damn fool. If his brothers could hear him. And for what? He'd made a fool of himself. Using words to compare her to some of the most beautiful things he'd ever seen as he'd traveled the country on his bike. She was a silent night when you needed peace.

Marley's hand raised to her neck, reaching for a phantom necklace before she'd dropped it. "I, uh, thank you. Even though it's not true. I appreciate the kind words."

He grunted and balled his fists behind his back. If she were his woman, he'd spank her for that. Lay her over his lap with his hard cock pressed against her stomach so she'd feel how beautiful he thought she was. While he spanked her bare bottom red until she believed it. But she wasn't his woman, so he kept his damn hands to himself.

"You still haven't told me why you're here." His voice was harsh, but he couldn't fucking help it.

She was driving him crazy. Her beautiful ass standing there doubting him. Doubting herself.

"I want a nipple ring."

His brow raised, and he tilted his head. Picturing

her scalloped chest.

"I don't have much nipple. But I thought with a piercing it would give me a little something to add to my design..." Her words trailed off at his stone face. "Fine, if you don't want to work with me anymore. I can ask one of the other guys..." She huffed and puffed her little kitten fur up, bristling.

He growled. "Hell no." Too harsh? Probably so, when he took in her open mouth and raised brows. "I'll do it. But I hope this isn't more bullshit about being beautiful. Because baby, you already got that covered."

Chapter 2

This was a mistake. What had she been thinking? Was it so wrong to want to feel beautiful again? She wanted to take off her shirt or dress, look in the mirror and think, *damn*. And here she was, standing in front of one of the most gorgeous men she'd ever seen in her life. Where had he been when she was single and whole? Now he was trying to convince her she still looked good. Not today. Maybe never again.

When she decorated her body with his art. She thought about the poem 'The Rose that Grew from Concrete. She wanted to be that rose, cracking concrete. Blooming again. She'd asked him to give her roses over the cracks of her scars. And he'd done it. Vining roses, blooming them across what little breasts she had left.

When she took off her shirt, she loved it. Smiled at herself. Sliding her hands across those delicate blooms and vines. And even the thorns. She hadn't asked for them, but the thorns were the best part. He'd gotten her. She wasn't trying to hide her battle

7

scars. She was trying to embrace them. At least she'd thought understood. But he looked so horrified when she asked for the nipple piercing. Was it so unheard of?

"Never mind."

"What the hell is that supposed to mean?"

"It means never mind. You don't wanna do this work. Maybe you're offended by my body art. Maybe you're judging me. I don't know why and I don't care. It's my body, and I'll enhance it anyway I want."

He mumbled a growl under his breath. So low she almost missed his words. "It doesn't need enhancing."

"What did you say?"

"I said there's nothing wrong with your body. You laid there while I painted your skin. The entire time I was working on you. I was hard as a bullet." Heat flared in his hazel eyes. Sparking little flames of green and gray. "That never happens to me. Anytime I'm working with a woman, I am a professional. She is a client. But with you every time I touched your skin. It felt like my hand would drop back and sizzle."

Her mouth dropped. Damn. That was how she'd felt.

"You made me burn. Baby, I burned."

Marley forced her mouth and tongue to close so that they could respond. "I don't know what to say to that."

He couldn't be serious. If he was, she hadn't picked up on that at all. He gave a half-smile. Half wicked sin, the other half boyish charm. The light in his eyes warming her.

"I guess you could say you felt the same. And that I made you burn. Did I, baby?"

Shit, he didn't know? She spent half the time laying on his table, pressing her legs together. Hoping he wouldn't see the wet spot growing between them. Yeah, he made her burn. For the last five years, she'd been busy fighting and then healing and then adjusting. No one had made her burn during those five years. They hadn't made her react like that before, if she was being honest. Should she admit it? Tell him?

She wanted to be a different Marley. Another reason for the tatt. She'd lived the first half of her life not taking any risks. Doing the right thing. Doing the safe thing. But when she beat death at his own game, she hadn't wanted to live her safe life anymore. What was the point in fighting for your life if you wouldn't live it? Nope, that was the old Marley. The new Marley, the resurrected Marley, knew what she wanted and wasn't afraid to say it.

"I burned hotter than a desert sidewalk in the summer." Her chocolate brown held his mysterious kaleidoscope-colored eyes.

Now what? He'd opened the door. And she'd

stepped her foot inside. But the hell if she knew what to do next. Did they just admit their attraction, smile, and politely go on about their day?

The colors in his kaleidoscope swirled faster than she would have imagined a man's eyes could change. But he said nothing. Holding her gaze until she needed to press her thighs together again. Until he stepped away from his tray table, walked towards her, and then passed her. Closing the door to the private room. Turning around to face her. She hadn't believed him when he said he'd burned. But damn, she saw it now. Flames leaping from his eyes like wildfire. Singeing her.

Rogue balled his fists, holding his hands stiffly at his side. "Come here."

His voice bridged the distance separating them. Commanding her with his rough, tentacled missive. Wrapping her in those two single words as if they were two tentacles pulling her closer.

"I wanted you from the first moment I saw you. But you were my client." He growled. "I don't make moves on my clients." He took her hands and pulled her closer to him. Searing a path across her knuckles with his thumbs. His eyes holding hers in his cage. "I wanted to pass you off to one of my brothers. But I was too fucking selfish. I didn't want anybody else seeing this."

He took his hands and opened her shirt. Releasing

the buttons one at a time. Pulling the sides apart and staring at his handiwork. His eyes opened and dilated. His breathing was ragged as he gulped down air.

"I've never seen anything so beautiful." He shook his head. "It's not you. It's not me. Something we created together. I could never have done this art for anyone else. You lay there like the bravest woman in the world, aweing me. You didn't say a word. Didn't need to. Your struggle was etched into your skin." He ran his hands over the thorns. "That's why I added this. I wanted to show that there is no beauty without pain."

She nodded her head. Sighing at the feel of his hands across her flattened chest. The softest touch stimulating her more than his words.

"I uh." She swallowed hard. "I wanted to say thank you."

"Then do it." Rogue's hands dropped to his side. His eyes pulling her in again.

She licked her lips. Staring at the temptation of him. Those perfect bows beckoning her. "Thank you."

Rogue shook his head. Arching his wicked brow. "You can do better than that."

Chapter 3

C ould she do better than a mumbled thank you? She sure looked like she wanted to find out. Marley's fingers landed on his chest, lighter than a baby bird perching on a limb. The tremble sent a soft vibration echoing down to his hard cock. She perched for a minute. Her eyes fluttering up to his. Waiting. Watching. He didn't like to rush a woman, but she was taking too damn long. He swooped down and took the kiss he wanted. From the first moment they met, he'd wanted to dive into those lips. Every time she'd taken her lips between her teeth and nibbled, he'd almost put his gun down and painted her tatts on with his tongue instead. It was a miracle he'd made it through her session. But he'd done it. He'd focused and finished.

When she walked out of the shop, he'd accepted that he probably would never see her again. The other brothers had taken him out for a beer. But the cold brew couldn't douse the flame she'd started. The fire had burned. She was a damn fool for walking back into his shop. And an even bigger fool for thinking he was going to let her go again.

He snaked his fingers into her hair. Gripping her skull. Nope, he was not letting her go. His tongue wrote his name in her mouth. Branding her as his. And giving him to her in exchange. The taste—better than he'd imagined. Like honey infused with cinnamon. How had he lived without this taste? Without this kiss? He backed himself up to the wall, inching her along, too. Bracing himself for her weight. As he ground her body into his. Chest against chest, breasts against breasts. He crawled into her mouth. She was everything. Her taste was everything. Oh God, he ran his hands over the curve of her ass and couldn't resist giving those globes a light spank. She moaned in response. Damn. He lifted her up. Her legs wrapped around his waist as he held her on the shelf of his palms. He could have rested her on the bench of his jutting dick, 'cause that's how freaking hard it was. He'd never wanted a woman like this before. And he never would again.

He carried her backward. Inching his way to the table and laying her down. He tensed when she froze.

"Wait. Stop."

Shit. He forced his dick to shut up and listen. Hell, forcing himself as well. *Remember Ruiz. Remember how he raised you. We don't take what a woman won't give.* Ruiz had taught him that when he first joined the Roarers fresh out of high school and looking for trouble. There'd been lots of groupies hanging around then. When the money was flowing because nobody cared how they got it. He looked down at her eyes glowing up at him. Cautious as a baby bird, fluttery as a butterfly.

He laid her down on the table and cupped her face. "What's wrong, baby?"

She shook her head, her curly locks blanketing the table. "I can't do this. That's not who I am. That's not why I came here. I thought I could. But I can't." Her hands pushed at the barrel of his chest, and he raised up.

Taking a deep breath and repeating Ruiz's words like a mantra. *Never take what a woman won't give.*

"You're still not telling me what's wrong, baby." He pulled back, holding the hands braced on his chest.

The tremble in them shot arrows into his heart, lancing his desire. Was she scared of him? He'd poured his soul into her tattoos. And now she was shaking like a leaf battered by an autumn wind. Did she think he would do anything to hurt her? That killed his desire. Killed him. Yeah, they'd have to take him out for something stronger than a beer after this. Damn. He stood up and pulled her up with him. Stepping back to give her some breathing room. Dammit, was she hyperventilating?

"Take a deep breath, baby. It's okay. I'm not going to hurt you."

Her eyes opened wider than a highway tunnel. "No. It's not you..."

She shook her head. Her hands reaching out again, but he dodged them. And her hands fluttered like a leaf dropping back to her lap.

He didn't want her fucking sympathy.

"Okay, I know how that sounds. But I don't usually do this. I don't go out and have one-night stands with random guys."

His head snapped back. What the fuck? "Who said this was a one-night stand? And I'm damn sure, not random."

"I mean, I just figured. I mean. We don't really know each other." Marley's head dropped. And she started telling her concerns to her lap. Refusing to look up.

"I learned everything I needed to know when you laid on my table under my guns."

Her eyes narrowed, and her nostrils flared. "Is that what this is about? You want to have a pity fuck to make the poor little scarred-up victim feel better? Is that what gets you off? Does making love to..." She waved her hand over her body. Her lip turning up as if it was imperfect. "Does making love to someone like me make you feel better? Feel superior?" Marley whipped her head around and shifted her legs like

15

she was about to leap off the table.

"Hell no." He gripped her thighs and held her still. "What the fuck are you talking about? Is that what you think? That's fucked up, baby." He took her chin and turned her face up. "My dick was harder than a Glock when you walked in the door. And I didn't know jack shit about your chest or your scars. When I saw them, it only made me want you more. Who doesn't want a warrior? Who doesn't want someone who survived a battle? And has the proof that they came out fighting. I'm a fucking fighter." He balled his fists up and held them in her face. "Look at my hands."

Her eyes darted down to his knuckles, and she gasped.

"You see these scars? That comes from years of fighting. Grew up in a house where my mom drank too much. And then passed out before my dad came home and beat the shit out of me, just because. As soon as I was big enough to fight his ass back, I did. Left the house at sixteen. But I never fucking gave up. Finished high school on my own. Hanging out at the gym at night. Because it was the only place open twenty-four hours. That's where these guys found me. And gave me a home. I started doing some shit, baby." He shook his head. No, he didn't want to go there with her. He wanted to keep their space clean. He took a deep breath and took a step back from the

ledge he was barely holding on to. "I don't think...,
well, let's just say I had to do some shit to survive. Put
in some work. That put more scars on these hands,
a couple of slashes on my chest. But I never fucking
gave up. 'Cause I'm a fucking fighter. And when I
saw you, I knew you were too. That's what I wanted.
That's what I've been looking for. Somebody to fight
by my side. Somebody to ride with me. No matter
where our fucking highway takes us. I've never had
sex out of pity." He couldn't stop another growl.
"I've never done anything out of pity." His words
were spitting out like gunfire, but whatever.

She needed to fucking understand.

"If somebody needs help, I help them. If somebody
won't help themselves, I move on."

What the fuck else was there to say? He stepped
back from between her legs. Yeah, he was going
to need something stronger than beer. He ran his
fingers through his hair. His eyes taking slow sips of
her while waiting for her to leave. She swung her legs
back and forth, but she didn't jump down. He folded
his arms across his chest. What was she waiting for?
He didn't have shit else to say.

Her voice was a soft husky whisper but strong
enough to penetrate the wall he was trying to build.
"I never thought of myself as a fighter. Always
thought I'd be one of those people who'd just give
up if something bad ever happened to me. I had a

quiet, loving home. I would see a boy like you in high school, and I would feel sorry for you. Wonder what I would do if I were in your place. I'd spare a few moments of pity and then go on with my day." She shrugged, but at least she wasn't talking to her lap anymore. Now her eyes held his. Rekindling the burn. "I think everybody takes a turn to have something bad happen to them. When it was my turn, I surprised myself. I surprised everybody I knew. 'Cause this cancer shit backed me up against the wall, but I came out swinging like I'd been prizefighting all my life. And that's when I knew. I *am* a fucking fighter. I wanted to wear those scars on my chest like medals."

Marley's gentle sigh bridged their slim distance. "I know I haven't fought your battles. But believe me, I've been in war. When you touched my body, I felt things I haven't felt in five long years. I meant what I said about not being a one-night stand. But if you're looking for someone to ride with you longer than that. I'm willing to see where this road takes us." She jumped down off the table. Her brow arched, and she pushed her shoulders back. Puffing out her beautiful chest. "If you still want to ride, that is?"

Chapter 4

F uck, he was glaring. But she needed to quit using his heart like balls on her Yo-Yo. Swinging him from one side to the other. Bouncing his heart around. Dammit, she needed to be sure.

"Be damn sure. Cause there's no going back from this. When someone joins up with us, they join for life. When I say I want you to be my woman, it's not a one-night deal. It's not a one-week deal. It's until we stop burning for each other. And that might never happen. So be damn sure."

She swallowed hard, probably gulping down her courage. Dammit, she wasn't sure. Not only was it going to take a strong drink. It was going to take several of them. He took a step back. Damn her. She took a step forward. He swung his arms backward, but she grabbed them. What the fuck?

"I'm sure."

His heart skidded to a stop. And then revved up and took off.

"I'm sure." Marley opened her mouth to repeat

it when he stood there like a wooden idiot. But she didn't need to get past the next 'I'm'.

Hell no. She didn't need to tell him again. He slammed his mouth down on hers, thrusting her words back into her mouth with his tongue. Grabbing the back of her head, tilting it into his kiss. Fuck. She was paradise. Nope, he wasn't ever going to stop burning for her. He grabbed the front of her shirt to rip it the rest of the way off her body when she lifted her hands to stop him. Damn it, had she changed her mind again? He'd told her to be fucking sure.

But she shook her head and whispered. Giggling at his confusion. "I can't walk out without a shirt."

Why was she still laughing? Maybe because he was standing there like a damn idiot again.

"We sell t-shirts out front, you can wear."

Marley's patient smile seared him. And he needed a deep breath to jump-start his heart again. Her smile was like lifting a helmet visor and looking into the sun. A rider could do it. But he'd be blinded for life. Never able to enjoy its warmth from any other source. Because no other source would ever compare. Shit.

"I'm sure you do." She slid the shirt down her arms. Folding it and placing it in a chair. "But let's save this one." She stared at her the neat creases, her fingers tracing over each fold while she bit her lip. "I haven't done this a lot. Okay, ever. But I'm pretty sure keeping your shirt is better than buying a new one."

Whatever. He grabbed her back into his arms. She didn't feel what he did. Didn't understand how he needed her. If she did, she wouldn't stand there calmly undressing. Not when all he wanted to do was snatch the clothes off her body. And leave them in rags on the floor. She wasn't there yet. But he was going to make sure she did. If he had to drag her by her hair. He pulled her closer. Ripping his shirt over his head. He had no problem walking out, butt-ass naked if he had to. And he didn't give a damn who realized what they had been doing. Everybody needed to know anyway. So they'd keep their fucking hands to themselves.

He snatched her back into his warmth. His body cold from the few seconds they'd been apart. He wrapped his arms around her and tried not to break her ribs. Grinding her chest into his. Doing his best to lift her tats onto his. She was so damn sexy. He cupped her ass and ground her hard against his erection.

She hissed.

Damn right.

"Feel what you're doing to me. That's after a few minutes in your company. Last time you tortured me for hours. Now it's my turn."

"Your turn?"

"You need to feel the torture I felt. Burn, like I

burned. Lay there so close to desire but out of reach. So close to coming, but stuck on the edge."

She wrapped her hand around his neck. Stilling his demand by looking up at him. Freezing him with her chocolate gaze. "We're edging? We're not coming?"

"You're going to come harder than you have in your life. Don't worry, baby. I wouldn't torture you like you did me."

"But you said..."

He pushed her back toward the table. It was too fucking small for what he had in mind. But they were gonna make it work. Because no way could they make it to his house. Not when he couldn't walk. Not while his third leg was dragging the ground between them. She still didn't get it. But he could show her better than he could tell her. Rogue pushed her protests down her throat with his kiss. Licking the sides of her tongue and playing tag between their two mouths. Sucking her back into his mouth like he hoped she'd suck his dick later. Much later.

"Lay down." He flattened her.

His dick rose higher when she responded to his command without fear. Some women grew anxious when a lover got a little growly, but not his woman. Her eyes lit up. She enjoyed it. She laid back and arched her eyebrows. Challenging him to bring it. Oh, hell yeah. Challenge accepted. He held her gaze in his firm grip while he unbuckled her jeans and slid them down her generous hips. Curves for days. He swallowed to keep his drool from dripping onto her belly.

His eyes broke away to skim along the curves and edges of her body. Because why should his hands have all the fun? They'd enjoyed themselves as they pulled the garment off, and the eyes wanted to join in the play. So did his mouth. He left the home he'd made in hers to taste the sides of her neck. What was that taste? So uniquely hers. It was sunshine peeking over the horizon. She tasted of the summer wind flowing over him on his bike. Salty when he rode by the ocean. Sweet when he flew past cornfields. He'd been riding since he was seventeen, but her taste was the first time he felt the same flying sensation of his bike. Damn. What was she doing to him?

Rogue's lips coasted down to the apex of her desire. Finding that she'd arrived before him. Her fingers calling shotgun on her clit. He swatted them away. They were too comfortable playing on his turf. He was claiming everything in the territory and was graffitiing the spot with wet kisses. Kisses that he blew on, to help the marks sink into her skin. He didn't bother with fancy words. He only needed one word. . Only one word counted. Mine. Mine. Mine. Mine. He worked the word into her skin with his lips, his tongue, and nips of his teeth.

Wresting the lips covering her clit apart to mark

that territory, too. He pushed his fingers in her mouth and let her sucking pull wet them before curling them into her pussy. Working his way into the tight passage and writing the word inside her quivering walls. Mine. He hadn't been possessive of anything in his life. The streets had taught him how easily a prized possession could be taken. That it was better not to get too attached to anything. But when she groaned his name. Her soft moan of 'Rogue' restructured his code. This was something to hold and keep. He'd never let that moan fall into another man's ears. It was his, dammit.

The thought had him jerking his head down to tongue-lash her pussy so she wouldn't forget who she belonged to. The rule was don't get possessive. But he was breaking it for his exception. She was the fucking exception. And he was gonna be possessive as hell. He hoped she didn't mind, but fuck it if she did. She was his. He knew it. Her pussy knew it, and her fucking heart better get on the same page real quick.

Her knees were roughing up the sides of his head. His muscles were bulging to hold her ass to the table and keep her from sliding off. But he wasn't going to stop. Not even when she started sounded as bat shit crazy as he felt. Her keening cries echoing around the room. Thank God for the satellite radio pumping throughout the shop for privacy. If anybody heard even a peep of her cries, they would know what the fuck was going on. He didn't fucking care, but his lady might not like it. And taking care of her, making sure she had the things she liked and wanted, had shot to the top of his things-to-do list.

Her stomach tensed, and her hips arched up on the table. Knocking his head back as she started to come. Shivering and shaking. Oh. Hell no. He pulled back and waited for her glistening eyes to find his. Reality settled back into her mind, even as she shook her head in protest.

"What..."

"Not yet. And not without me. I've been dreaming about this, day and night since you left. Callouses on my hands from yanking on my dick. Changing the sheets every night and waking up with cold showers like a damn adolescent. So, not fucking yet."

He yanked his pants down and tried not to trip over his shitkickers. Stomping across the room to grab a condom out of a drawer. Her eyes were big. Either from the sight of his pole or his agitation as he pulled the condom on. He waved her down off the table.

"Get down. Turn around and bend over." He shot the rough commands out. He should be smoother. But fuck smoothness. He had to get balls deep inside her. Right. Damn. Now.

Her skin shivered when he traced the curve of her spine. Enjoying the view and telling his dick to slow down before he came all over her fucking back. She couldn't see his expression, which sucked for her. But she didn't need to see how fucking crazy he was right now. If she saw his face, she would get a view of madness. He took a deep breath. He was too fucking hard. Too fucking scary. Calm the fuck down. Act like a fucking gentleman or at least a man. Put the monster away.

He kissed her butt cheek. Nibbling the curve of each globe and digging his fingers back into her tight channel. Scissoring them to widen and prepare her for his entry. Shit, she was tight.

He leaned forward. Kissing his way up her spine to the curve of her cheek. "You ready, baby?"

She nodded. Taking a deep breath to meet his lips and salute his tongue. Damn. That was what he needed. A tender sweet to soothe the beast. He took his dick and flagged it up and down her slit. Wresting more moisture from her passage before nudging his way in. Her breath hitched, and he froze.

"Still with me, baby?"

She nodded. He would have pulled back at that weak-ass reply. But she arched her neck and pulled him back into her kiss. Giving him more of her sweetness as he inched his way inside. Sometimes a piercing would close up, and a client would request a new hole. He would explain that the hole only needed to be gently worked apart. And that's what he did. He wormed his way into her hole. Reminding her body of how much pleasure her pussy could hold, feel, and give. He clung to her kiss. Giving soft nudges in and out. Marley's body curled around him. Fluid and relaxed as it welcomed him.

She sighed. Releasing him from the kiss with a soft mew of pleasure.

"You still good, baby? Tell me, you're still good"

"More than good." She sighed again when he gave another shallow plunge. She buried her forehead in the table.

He slid back. Bracing his arms above her and caging her under his body. He pulled back and enjoyed the tug her pussy held on his dick as it resisted his exit.

"Don't worry, sweet puss, I'm coming back." And he did.

He slammed back into her. Checked to see how she was handling his rough. But his lady was a rider. He slammed into her again, forcing out another sharp breath release. Their grunts mixed and merged. Rogue picked up speed. Battering into her. Drilling in his desire. Firing up her pussy with his meat stomping all over her walls. He moved his hands to the curve of her ass to hold her as he slammed into her over and over. Ignoring the pool gathering on them. He wiped the sweat away from his eyes so he wouldn't miss her ass jiggling with his pounding.

His hips started slowing. No dammit, not yet. Her pussy started bucking to encourage his new rhythm. Both of them, arching and rubbing, grinding and pounding, sweating and cursing their way to climax.

"Shit. Shit. Shit. Mine, Mine. Mine."

And under it all. After it all. It was her moaned response That finally yanked him over the edge.

"Yours. Yours. Yours."

Forcing him to yield and release. Pumping stream after stream into her body. He'd never hated a condom more, as she came around his gloved limb. Shuddering around his dick before arching herself off the table and collapsing. Damn. Shit and Fuck. He collapsed on her back and melded into her body.

Chapter 5

"Baby, it doesn't take that long to button up a shirt. What's wrong?"

It was easy for him to stand there looking smug and satisfied. Rogue's eyes glowing with satisfaction. But he didn't have to do the walk of shame through the shop and out to her car. Her face flushed with heat, thinking about what they'd done. What the others in the shop could have heard.

"Any way we could stay in here until the shop closed?" Marley mumbled the question. While trying to work the buttons on her shirt with all the dexterity of a two-year-old.

His enormous hands engulfed hers. Steadying their tremble. And using their enclosed hands to lift her chin. Forcing her to meet his gaze.

"Is that what's bothering you? Worrying about my brothers?"

"I'm not worried. But they probably heard everything. We weren't exactly quiet."

His brow furrowed. She tried to tug her hands away,

but he wasn't having it.

"Who cares? I'm not embarrassed. And I'm damn sure not ashamed. You're my lady now. I think they're grown enough to figure out what we're doing when we're alone. Believe me, if they think anything about us, they'll be thinking he's a lucky son of a bitch." Rogue dropped her hands to cup her face. His thumbs holding her cheeks while his fingers dug into her hair. "'Cause that's how I feel. They may look like a bunch of rough and tumble guys. But every single one of them wishes they had a lady of their own." His thumbs pulled the lip she'd been nibbling on out of her mouth. And laced it with a feathery soft kiss. He drew in a deep breath at her silence. "But if you don't feel the same. If you're embarrassed by me..."

"No. God, no." Marley grabbed his hands. "It's just they're your friends. And like I said, I haven't done this a lot. Hell, I haven't done this at all in years. Feels a little awkward. If we're going to be together. I wanna make a good impression." She took a deep, shaky breath. Steadying her shoulders and holding on to his sturdy frame. "I mean, you call them your brothers. So, it's like meeting your family for the first time."

"You don't have anything to worry about. Putting this jacket on your shoulder tells them everything they need to know about you. If you wear my colors, that means you're my ride-or-die. I look out for you no matter what. And they will too. Never had anyone wear my colors."

"Your colors?"

Rogue swung the leather jacket off the hook by the door. Turning her around and placing the jacket on her shoulders. It swallowed her up like some teeny-bopper cheerleader wearing the star quarterback's letterman jacket. She would have reeled from its heavy weight if he hadn't held her steady.

"My colors. Ruiz gave me this jacket when I was nineteen. I was still scrawny then, and it swamped me. Same as you. But he knew I'd grow into it. I'd been hanging around the club for two years before they made me official. Once I got my colors, I never let anybody get near it. Almost died to keep it a couple of times, but I didn't care. I earned this jacket by being a soldier. Someone willing to fight to the end. Just like you."

Tears blurred her vision, but like a real soldier, she forced them to stand down.

"And you want me to have it?" The husky question stumbled on its way out.

She couldn't accept it. It was too much.

"No." He laughed at her surprise.

Had she misunderstood? He hadn't offered it to her. What was going on?

"I want you to wear it. Keep it on; show it off. Hold

on to it while I get you your own jacket. You fight your own battle. You get your own medal. That's what the jacket reps." He pulled it from her shoulders to show her. "Everybody's jacket means something different. See, mine has this..."

She squinted at the intricate design. A skull with two bones... She squinted harder. "Wait, are those two wrenches?"

"You're good. Many people don't get it. But I'm the mechanic. The one they came to when they'd be cut up and bleeding. I'm the one who puts things back together. I enjoy fixing people."

She bit her lip. Damn... "Like me?"

His eyes widened before he shook his head. His words were gruff as he pulled her into his arms. "No, you didn't need fixing. If anything, you're fixing me."

Yeah right. "How?"

"Showing me that there are still good and beautiful people in the world. When you give me you, it's like you're surprising me with a bouquet of roses. I love your tattoo. It's perfect for you. You're my bouquet of roses."

She crinkled her nose at him. "You're kind of corny for a tatted-up biker guy. You know that, right?"

He arched his brow and snatched her up in one swoop. Forcing her laughter out in unladylike snorts. Oh God, she hadn't laughed like that in years.

"Corny my ass. Wait 'til I get you home. I'll give you something better to do with that mouth than sass me."

She shook her head and patted his chest. "Still corny, big guy, but keep right on trying. Ow," she clenched her butt cheeks at his swat. "What was that for?"

"When I smarted off at school, the nuns would give me a swat."

"And I bet you loved it."

"I bet you will too. Let's get the fuck out of here. I need to teach you a few things..."

"So, you're a teacher now?"

"Only for you, baby girl. Let's go."

She was still laughing when they entered the lounge area of the shop. As soon as they entered, all conversation ceased. Shit. It was as if someone had shut the lights off, and everyone stood in stunned silence. Shit. She wiggled for release, but he tightened his grip. His voice rumbled out of his chest.

"I'm shutting down for tonight. I'll catch up with you guys tomorrow." He looked down and grabbed her gaze. "I'll probably be late. Rector, can you cover me if I'm not in by noon?"

Her body was on fire. Her face flushing redder than the crimson flame tattoo on the shop's door. Why wouldn't he put her down? Why wasn't she melting into the floor? She raised her glance enough to see one of the other artists put down his equipment and approach them. He nodded.

His smoky voice matched his gray eyes. "No problem. You know I keep my schedule free for subbing and office work. I got you." His eyes sliced over to hers like knives. "Are you going to introduce us to your young lady?"

"Kind of in a hurry to get her home." His gruff answer had her wiggling harder, trying to jump out of his unyielding arms. "This is Warrior."

Oh Lord. She lifted her head to correct her name from around his bulging biceps. "Marley."

Rector's eyebrow arched up to his bald hairline. "Ah, the young lady you told me about. The one that got away?"

He nodded. "But she came back, and I'm keeping her."

People died of embarrassment, didn't they? Was that a real thing or not? Because if it was, she should be pushing up daisies. Especially when the whooping and hollering started up. Making the shop sound more like a raunchy bachelor party than a tattoo shop. Rogue swung around and she faced the shop.

Ignoring her wiggles and her red blotchy face, he introduced her. "Guys, this is Marley. She just agreed to be my lady."

Did she agree to that? When had that happened?

She huffed up into his face to challenge him. But he looked so damn happy. Like a kid who opened his present on Christmas and found the shiny red bike or the new puppy he'd been begging for. It was official. She had joined him in the corny zone because she couldn't take his red bike away. And she didn't freaking want to. No, she wanted him to look this happy always. Because that's how she felt. Only she didn't have the courage to show it. Or did she?

"What do you say Marley, are you his lady? Cause if not, and you're looking for somebody a whole hell of a lot better looking, look over here."

"Shut up, Rebel. She doesn't need a pretty boy. Do you, baby?"

"Yes, I do. And I got him. Right here. Everything I wanted and all I need." She patted his chest again before snuggling into his hold. Ignoring the cheers and laughs.

"Everything I need and all I want." He repeated her words. He mixed them up, but hell, who cared? Not her. Not with the sincerity and wonder showing in his eyes. "You ready to go, my corny baby?"

"Hell yeah." She answered. "Let's go, baby." But whispered the last… "so we can start coming."

Epilogue

Two months later...

Marley bit her lip to stop herself from crying. Both drove Rogue crazy. No crying, no biting, as if he could command her emotions like he did her body. She shoved her hands under her thighs to stop the shaking that she couldn't help. She couldn't go through this again. They were just starting their lives together. And it was all going to be taken away. Shit, she hated this.

His eyes narrowed. "Calm down, it's going to be okay." He pulled her hands into his. He really believed it. As if believing it would make it true.

But he didn't know what she had been through. The waiting was the tough part. Much, much worse than not knowing. Two weeks of phantom pain shooting through her breasts. Terrifying her. It wasn't all the time, a weird twinge here and there. It was the persistence that had her shaking. She'd tried to hide it from him. Tried pretending he didn't know her body better than she did. But when he'd kissed her nipple, and she'd winced, he'd forced her to make the appointment. It was just a little grunt, but he saw her. He always did. Her eyes teared. Dammit, she should have done this by herself. But she couldn't, and she wouldn't have been able to hide it from him, anyway. That was the problem with having somebody always up in your face. Not willing to give her space. She should have done this with Belle.

"Stop that. They told you don't worry, so don't. And no matter what happens, I got you. We got this."

She crushed his hands in a death grip. Surprised, she didn't break his fingers with her clasp. But instead of complaining, he brought her hands to his lips. Kissing them.

"I got you. I'm here. No matter what, we'll get through this."

She took a deep breath and forced her grip to relax.

How would they get through it? It had drained her parents. Drained her friends. She wouldn't put him through the same torture. She'd have to run away. No other way he would let her go. Maybe it would be a short remission. She'd take the medicine. Survive again and then come back. Whole and healthy, like he'd met her.

His eyes captured hers, holding her gaze as tightly as she held his hands.

"If anything happens. If I−."

"–Nothing's going to happen. We're in this to-gether. Ride or die. Warriors to the end." Rogue's nostrils flared and his eyes narrowed. "Remember who you are. Who we are. I love you, Marley. You are my entire world. My universe. Everything in my life spins around your sun. So, nothing is going to happen to you. Nothing *can* happen to you. You got that?"

If only it was that simple.

"Miss Thomas? We're ready for you." The pretty blonde nurse with her perfect breasts gave a pla-cating smile. Easy to do when her world wasn't crashing.

Marley wasn't jealous. She wasn't that type of girl. Was she? *No, so stop it.* She took a deep breath. The nurse gave Rogue a lustful once over as they passed by. *Whoa, back up, I'm not dead yet.* She rolled her eyes, even though Rogue didn't notice. All his thoughts, his focus, his concentration was on her. As it had been since they'd met two months earlier. He never wavered. No, she didn't have any reason to be jealous. He took her hand and pulled her into the office, settling them down on their chairs. She didn't want to jump up on the examination table. Just looking at it made her nauseous. Her hand slicked with sweat, and she started to withdraw it. But he only squeezed her hand tighter. Hell, was he nervous too?

38

Doctor Rami walked in. She loved Doctor Rami. Her wise, kind eyes had helped Marley through hard days and decisions. She wore her salt and pepper hair in a long thick braid that traced down back. Her brown skin was warm as nutmeg. The same color as her mom's. She'd been a good doctor. She'd been a good friend. Too bad they'd met under these circumstances. When terror turned their friendship into resentment.

Rogue squeezed her hand. How did he know? He always knew. God, she loved him so much. His words echoed in her head even though he never moved his lips. *You're a warrior. We're warriors in this together. Ride or die. Ride or... die.* Damn.

"Well, Marley, I got your test results back from your blood work. I'm glad you came in as soon as you did. Because we need to run some more tests and get you started on some medication." She paused, her eyes flicking to Rogue. "You told the nurse it was okay to talk in front of this gentleman."

Gentleman had a question mark. Any other time, Marley would have smiled. Everybody had the same reaction to her big, bad biker. Rough and tough-looking in his club colors. His face full of grim determination made him look a little angry. But it was all love. Concern. She squeezed his hand.

"Yes, it's okay to talk in front of him. More than okay."

The doctor nodded and opened the file. "In that case, I have the results of your blood work here and I think it's best if I just hand them to you."

Okay, that was new. Maybe she didn't want to speak in front of Rogue. She took the file, perusing the test results. Her blood count was in the normal range, white blood count was also normal. Whew, thank God. The white blood count was the one that you had to look out for. That meant it couldn't be too bad, right? She kept looking down. Normal range hCG. She looked up her brow arching.

"hCG? That's a new one. What does hCG measure? What does it mean?"

The doctor beamed a smile too bright for an office. Her joy was unprofessional and exuberant. Marley's brow furrowed even more.

"It means you're pregnant."

Marley's jaw dropped. She must have misunderstood. Her mouth started working open and close, but speech was impossible. Now Rogue was the one squeezing too tight. Squeezing her hand so hard, her fingers almost cracked. But she couldn't look at him. *What...*

Dr. Rami repeated herself as if talking to a child. "It means you are pregnant."

"But, I can't be. I've been feeling something strange with my breasts. But I thought it meant a tumor might be behind the nipple. I thought it meant something..."

Dr. Rami laughed. They'd shared a lot of tears in the office, not a lot of laughs. "It does mean something. It means you are pregnant. Pregnancy can cause changes in your breasts and your nipples. These changes are all normal signs of an early stage in pregnancy. A very good and healthy sign."

Tears flooded her eyes, her lashes the gatekeepers holding them back. "But am I healthy? Is it a healthy pregnancy? Am I going to be okay? Is he..." Her hands wrapped around her belly. Already protective of the life they covered. Already willing to do anything to save this life. Even more than her own.

Rogue wrapped his hands around hers. Protecting their child and her. Holding them both in his grasp. She loved his rich baritone bass. The deep voice always sent chills down her spine and made her panties soaking wet. But this was a tone she'd never heard before.

His voice was cracking and fragile. "Is she going to be okay? Are they both going to be okay? The priority is Marley. You understand that. I need them both to be alright."

"They are both fine. And they're both going to be okay. We will monitor her closely. Have her come in for a few extra tests and ultrasounds. I want her to start prenatal vitamins right away." She rattled off a quick list, looking at Marley. "They're very important. Drink plenty of fluids." She turned her head back to Rogue. "Make sure she stays hydrated. She should get most of her nutrition from vegetables and fruits. You don't want to spoil her too much."

"Never. I couldn't spoil her too much, Doc. She's everything."

The doctor's eyes fluttered, and she turned to Marley like, *wow.* Marley gave a slight nod, beaming. *Exactly, see why I'm keeping him?* Marley communicated with her eyes. The doctor nodded.

"Well, I meant with the sweets. Pregnant women tend to want fatty foods, ice cream, milkshakes, and cookies. That's natural, too. Nature's way of telling us to stay relaxed and get comfortable. But these things in moderation are okay. Especially chocolate or any other type of caffeine."

Marley shook her head because she knew how his mind worked, too. And she could see the upcoming fights. She was not giving up chocolate. The doctor said in moderation. Dr. Rami handed her a script for the vitamins.

Rogue took it out of her hands. "I'll take care of this. I'll take care of everything."

"It's good to see you again, Marley." She looked back and forth between Marley and Rogue and sighed. "I'm so happy for you."

Marley nodded again. She was doing that a lot. It

was all the shock allowed.

She took a shaky breath when the doctor left. "Oh, my God. I'm pregnant".

He corrected, "*We* are pregnant."

She nodded, the tears coming again. "I never thought in a million years... I didn't know... I didn't ask her about breastfeeding..."

"It doesn't matter. Nothing matters. Healthy is all we need. My two healthy girls."

"We don't know if it's a girl."

"Yeah, it wouldn't be anything else. An angel for my angel."

"I should have asked you how you felt about it? I know you didn't have this in mind..."

He smirked. His wicked wink made her laugh. "Who says I didn't?"

"Oh, you planned this? Without asking me?"

"I thought you got it every time I sprayed my name inside your walls."

Marley flushed, hoping the nurse couldn't hear them.

"Do you think I've ever been bare-backed with anybody else?" He shook his head. "Nobody but you. You're the only one I ever wanted to carry my child. It is my honor. It is my pleasure. I don't have the words. *Nobody* has the words to tell you how happy I am. You're healthy, you're *both* healthy, and I'm the happiest guy in the world. I love you already, with every piece of myself. I didn't know I had more love to give. But I guess I do. I already love this baby, too. How do you feel about it?" His brows drew together, and he clasped her shoulders. "I mean, I know I come from a rough background, and I had shit for parents. But I swear to you, Marley. I swear with everything I am. On my colors... I. Will. Do. Better. Give this baby everything I am. Do everything I can to make sure she has a perfect life. The one you both deserve."

Marley pulled his face down to kiss away the salty silver tracing down his cheeks. "The life we all deserve. Now, stop all this corny crap. Please don't tell me you're going to be even cornier for the next few months." She kissed him again. Wrapping her arms around him and holding on before dropping back.

"Of course, I am." He lengthened the quick smack, diving deeper into her warm mouth before releasing her. Resting his forehead on hers. "Let's go. We got some celebrating to do."

"To the shop?"

"In private, at least right now."

"Mmm, sounds good to me."

She heard the nurse call as Rogue opened the door. "Congratulations, Miss Thomas!."

She turned around to say thank you.

Rogue's brash voice, deep and masterful, stopped her. "That's the last time she'll call you that."

"Call me what?"

"Miss Thomas. I'll be changing that as soon as possible." He leaned down and stole another kiss. "As soon as possible..."

Choosing Her - Skin Sins Book 2

Continue Reading for a Sneak Peek at the sexy follow up to Skin Sins Book 1

Belle Walters chewed her nail when she walked into Skin Sins. Dammit, where was Marley? Probably in the back with her hot biker. She wasn't jealous. Hell no, she was living vicariously through her bestie's life. And if anyone deserved a sexy surprise love life, it was Marley. She still remembered when Marley struggled to make it home because she was so sick. Terrifying Belle out of her mind. Wondering if her best friend since kindergarten would make it. But she'd pushed her fears aside and did everything she could do to support her. And now five years later, look at her. Not everybody got a happy ending after such a terrifying diagnosis. It was a great happy ending. Belle would never have thought, looking at Rogue, that he was the kind of guy to dote on a girl. But he was. True, it meant a lot of their late-night girl dates had ended. But he always welcomed Belle when she came around. Thoughtful enough to leave the room if they needed private time. Never leaving without giving Marley the sweetest kiss and the softest look. When he left, they would press their hands over their hearts and sigh. Then giggle like high schoolers. Careful to keep laughter low so that he wouldn't know they were making fun of him. But tonight was their night. He'd promised them they could have this tonight. Claiming he didn't know how he was going to make it without Marley. But that he would try. Saying it was the least he could do after holding her best friend captive for an entire month. She sighed again. She was starting to love the guy almost as much as Marley did. She didn't usually trust his type. But he was changing her mind about bad boy bikers. Not that she had to worry. No guy like that would ever want her. And she wouldn't believe him if he did. Gorgeous bad-boys didn't fall for her. They sensed the school teacher a mile away. And with her thunder thighs, there was no way she would get on a bike and ride around town with him like Marley did.

Stone's Throw buzzed with excitement when the group of tatted-up bikers had settled in the town. Talk of sex trafficking and drug-running kept the rumor mills going more than the old sawmill ever had. There'd even been a rumor that Brad had stopped in to give them an official law enforcement warning. But if he did, nothing ever came of it other than his new tattoo. After his tat, a lot of people were walking around town with their fresh ink. Even some of the kids in her A.P. lit class had ink. But this was her first time visiting the shop. She'd smelled the testosterone from the sidewalk before she'd entered. Tired of waiting for Marley in her car. She'd gathered up her courage and opened the door. Walking into the shop she'd heard so much about. It was nicer than she'd expected. Reminding her of a fancy beauty salon. The front part of the shop faced the street with a big picture window. Comfy-looking couches, magazines, a big screen tv with a video game system filled the area. Everything to make a person comfortable, if they needed to wait a long time. Even a mini-fridge and coffeemaker, yeah this was nice. She could have been waiting in here the whole time. An unattended reception desk, with a computer and appointment book, divided the space. Looking past it, the room went from cozy comfort to pristine professional. Clean white-tiled workstations held shiny equipment and supplies. No wonder they were building a good rep despite their hell-raiser looks.

They still hadn't noticed her. Some were working, some were talking, or cleaning. Everyone looked busy. She hated interrupting, but... She lifted her hands, but then forced her fingers down and scowled at her nails. Another manicure ruined. She'd hoped that by paying for expensive manicures, she would finally stop biting her nails. But she couldn't help it. She took a deep breath and cleared her throat. "Hi, I'm looking for Marley."

Six stares swiveled in her direction as if a zookeeper had walked into the lion's cage. She'd seen it happen once on a school field trip. The lions were in their outdoor enclosure, relaxing on their various rocks. Sunning themselves with lazy adoration. Until the zookeeper walked in. Their heads turning to her, as they got lazily to their feet. Their gold and amber eyes stalking her as she walked in with their meat. She'd thought the woman had to either be crazy as a Betsy bug or braver than a Navy SEAL. She hadn't been able to decide at the time. But now she was the one entering the enclosure with large predators, and oh yeah, that lady was nuts.

Of course, it was the largest scariest one who spoke

first. She zipped her eyes past the bulging muscles, to the silver eyes watching her. His stone visage giving away nothing. His voice was deeper than the ocean when he responded. Nodding his head towards the back. "She's with Rogue right now. I would say go back there, but nobody wants to interrupt them. Nothing you can do when they're back there going at it, other than wait."

"Umm, okay." She felt the heat rise up in her face. What could she say to that? Her best friend was in the back getting it on with her, um, boyfriend. Lover? She didn't know what to call him. Meanwhile, what was she supposed to do? She started nibbling her nails again. The first round was going to be on Marley. Making her wait and embarrassing her. Oh yeah, not only was the first round on her, but she was getting the appetizers also.

"If you need a place to wait," a sexy voice called from the back of the shop. The first guy's voice was deep. But something about the second guy. His voice shimmied down the length of her spine. Evoking a primordial response, eliciting goosebumps. She loved shifter romance books and it's like she was in one. The voice making her body respond as if he was her fated mate. Okay Belle, you've been reading one too many of those books. Shake it off. She strained her neck around the Goliath in front of her to get a glimpse of the face behind the voice. The voice called to her and her whole body responded. "You can come over here and sit on my chair. Or forget the chair and settle down on my lap." His words powered down the weird reaction. And she shook her head. Another immature ass with creepy one-liners. She handled high school boys and their trash lines all day. And nine-to-five was more than enough. She would never deal with that immature crap outside of school hours. What did he look like, anyway? She strained her neck a little harder. Who was it? Not that it would have made a difference. Marley had told her a little bit about some of the guys. But she wouldn't have been able to identify them from their voice.

"Ignore Rebel. We have a nice waiting section over there." The Goliath pointed to the carpeted area in front of the reception desk.

Rogue made his way between the chairs and the other tattoo artists towards her. Wiping his hands on a shop towel before wrapping it around his neck. His slow saunter stalking her like a beast in a zoo. She wiped her sweaty hands on the side of her jeans. If she had a piece of meat she would throw it at him to distract him and run for help. But he was looking at her as if *she* was the meat. "You don't wanna sit there, sugar." He was close enough now to smell his heady aroma. Damn, he was fine. Like movie star fine. Marley had shared that most of the guys came from a rough background. And they'd conducted some shady activities. But then something happened, and they'd decided to go straight. They'd moved to Stone's Throw and opened up a tattoo shop. Marley hadn't shared the details with her. She might not have the details. She pulled her lip into her mouth and gave it a quick nip. He groaned. Okay, what was that about? "Damn baby, you're killing me."

Goliath's voice rang out making her jump. How has she forgotten about him? Oh yeah, because of the hot guy standing in front of her swamping her senses with his sex appeal. And heaven help her, she was drowning in it. She knew better. Knew he was feeding her his well-practiced lines. But she was still drowning, unable to catch her breath. Damn, he was good. "Cut it out, Rebel." Goliath commanded. "You heard her say she's a friend of Marley's."

Rebel grinned and winked. "Well, you know what they say, any friend of hers is a friend of mine. You wanna be my friend, sugar?"

Will Rebel win the curvy school teacher with his foolishness? One thing's for sure - One of them is about to get schooled...

About the Author

I really hope you enjoyed *Cherishing Her.* My name is Jailaa West and I am an indie author of sweet steamy romance novels. I grew up In Chicago, Il. And I have loved romance books since junior high school when I snuck my first one from my mom's bookshelf. I used to dream about the fantasy worlds I read about. Now I enjoy writing them for others to dream about. As a mom of three, I frequently write after bedtime or behind a locked bedroom door. And I thank God that all of my hot steamy books, (that I still read and write) are stored safely on my tablet, where no one can sneak them off of my bookshelf!

You can connect with me on:

🌐 https://jailaawest.com

Subscribe to my newsletter:

✉ http://eepurl.com/hmBvhn

Also by jailaa west

Meet the Men and Women of Savage Security
They Protect your Body. You Protect your Heart.

These sweet steamy hot romances will get your heart pumping from the romantic suspense. These men are determined to save and protect their women.

Will Alana forgive Colt? Only if she **Submits**...

Can Beau Save Ella? He will if she **Obeys**...

Can Adam keep Daysha? Only if he's in **Control**...

Will Aiden win Cassie? Only if she **Yields**...

Skin Sins MC Tattoo Shop
Love, Lust & Ink

These tough ex-bikers walked away from a life of crime. These lovely ladies are showing them that passion pays more than sin.

Skin Sins is a short steamy series of standalone books with a guaranteed HEA and no cliffhanger or cheating. The mature content is not for the faint of heart.

Free with Kindle Unlimited

After the Ball - Modern Day Fairy Tales
Yours Until Midnight - Modern Day Cinderella

Every woman deserves to be Cinderella at the ball at least once in her life. At least that's what Taylor tells herself when she sneaks into Carter Strong's fundraising ball. No one's going to notice her. Right? Until he does. Now she has until midnight to have a no-strings-attached night of passion with a man who captures her heart.

Loving the Beast - Modern Day Beauty and the Beast

Nella only wanted to return Bryson *The Beast* Dufort's stolen candelabra. Does he repay her with thanks and eternal gratitude? No, of course not, not when he's known to the world as *The Beast*. Now he's forcing her to choose between a fake engagement and jail.